For information address HarperCollins Children's Books, a division of HarperCollins Publishers, 195 Broadway, New York, NY 10007.
www.harpercollinschildrens.com
ISBN 978-0-06-294114-5

The illustrations and hand lettering were drawn by hand on a digital device.

20 21 22 23 24 SCP
10 9 8 7 6 5 4 3 2 1

First Edition

For Nina

FRANKENSTEIN DOESN'T WEAR EARMUFFS!

JOHN LOREN

HARPER

An Imprint of HarperCollinsPublishers

Upon a haunted Halloween,
in deepest dungeon lair,

awakens monstrous **Frankenstein**
to give you all a scare.

Beneath a grim and ghostly sky,
the moon alight with fright,

Frankenstein emerges
on a dark and stormy—

HOLD IT!

Not so fast there, Frankenstein.
Those clouds are looking iffy.
So take my old galoshes here;
they're waterproof and spiffy.

BLOP blop blop blop blop blop blop op

In giant red and floppy boots
that just don't fit him right,

Frankenstein emerges
on a dark and stormy—

HANG ON!

In giant red and floppy boots
with earmuffs **way** too bright,

Frankenstein emerges
on a dark and stormy—

HEY,
WAIT!

In giant red and floppy boots,
with earmuffs way too bright,
a puffy orange parka
and a heavy camping light,
some smelly stripy tube socks
and a f

There's no dungeon that can hold him!
Your earmuffs are no use!

For Halloween's begun at last,
and Frankenstein is loose!

But the wind is really whipping . . .
it's pretty dark and foggy.

His Franken-tummy's grumbling . . .
his shoes are getting soggy.

Now his ears are feeling frosty,
and he starts to Franken-think
that maybe this year's Halloween
will really Franken-stink.

Look! The witch has woolly mittens,
and the werewolf's got a sweater.
The ghosts have fuzzy hats on . . .

. . . and he feels a little better.

So Frankenstein wore earmuffs
on that night so grim and ghostly.
And dark and stormy Halloween
was pretty warm and toasty.